Missing mummy

Rebecca Cobb

MACMILLAN CHILDREN'S BOOKS

Some time ago we said goodbye to Mummy.

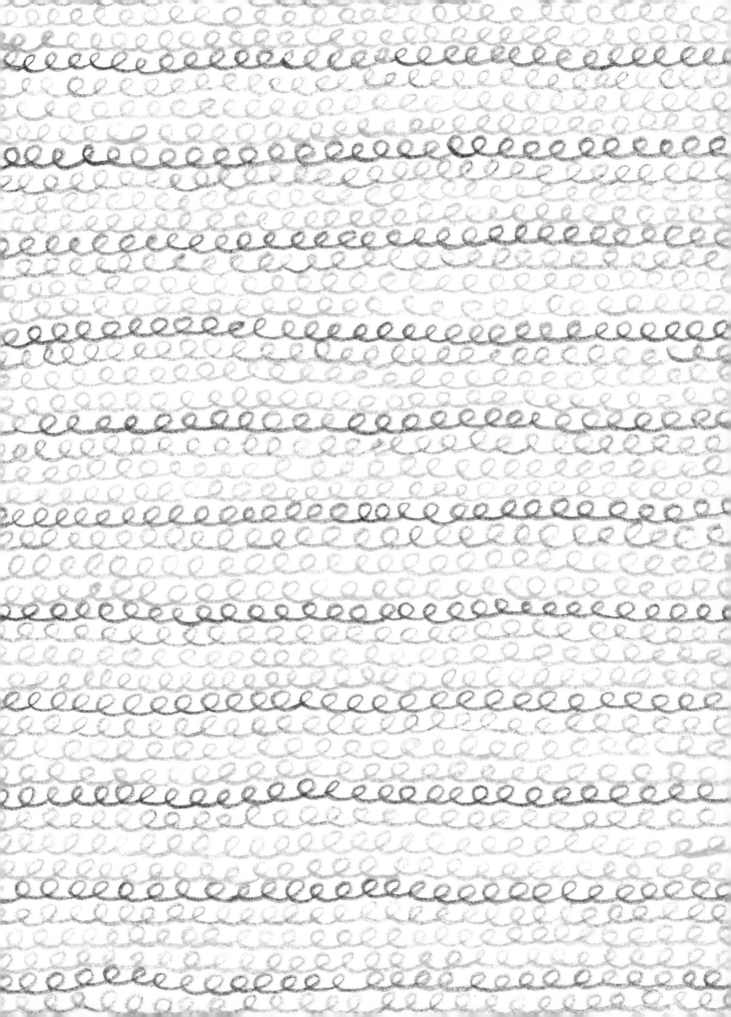

Thank you Mum and Richard, Sam, James, Ron and Louise;
thank you also to Jenni Thomas for all her help – RC

First published 2011 by Macmillan Children's Books
This edition published 2012 by Macmillan Children's Books
a division of Macmillan Publishers Limited
20 New Wharf Road, London N1 9RR
Basingstoke and Oxford
Associated companies throughout the world
www.panmacmillan.com

ISBN: 978-0-230-74951-1

Created with the professional advice and
kind support of the Child Bereavement Charity
www.childbereavement.org.uk

1 3 5 7 9 8 6 4 2

A CIP catalogue record for this book is available from the British Library.

Printed in China

I am not sure where she has gone.

I have tried looking for her.

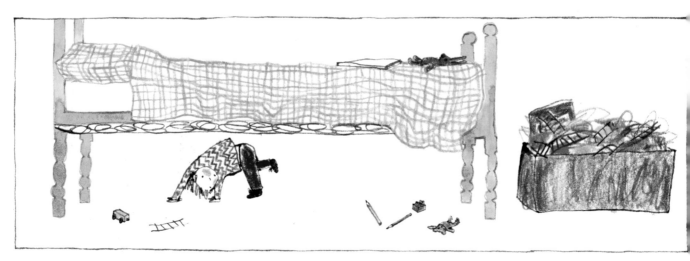

I found lots of her things.

She must have forgotten to take them with her.

We have been leaving her flowers . . .

. . . but she doesn't seem to
have been collecting them.

I feel so scared because I don't
think she is coming back.

And then I feel angry because I really
want her to come back.

I am worried that she left
because I was naughty sometimes.

The other children have *their* Mums.
's not fair.

I asked Daddy when Mummy
was coming back.

Daddy gave me a hug and told
me that Mummy had died.

He said you cannot come back once you have died
because your body doesn't work any more.

Daddy says it was nothing I did that made Mummy die.

He wishes she was here too, but we are still a family.

I am glad I have people to care for me.

We can talk about things we remember.

Together we look at photographs
which make us laugh and cry.

And we help each other to try and do all
the things Mummy used to help with.

Daddy says I do them very well.

I really miss my Mummy.

But I will always remember her.

I know how special I was to my Mummy and she will always be special to me.

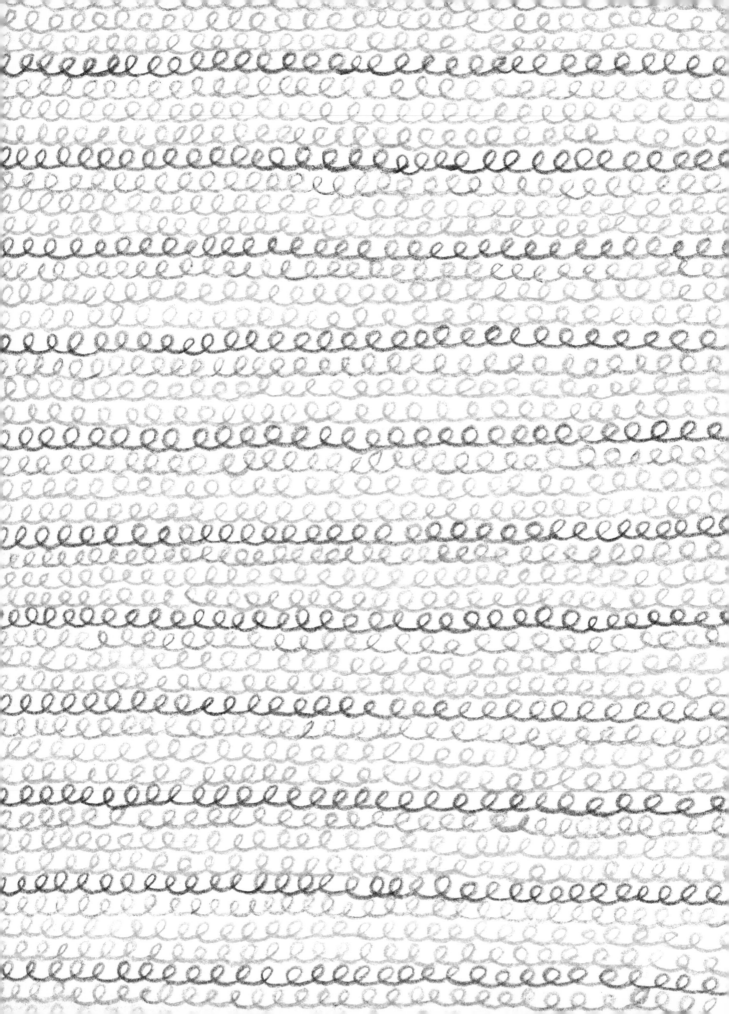

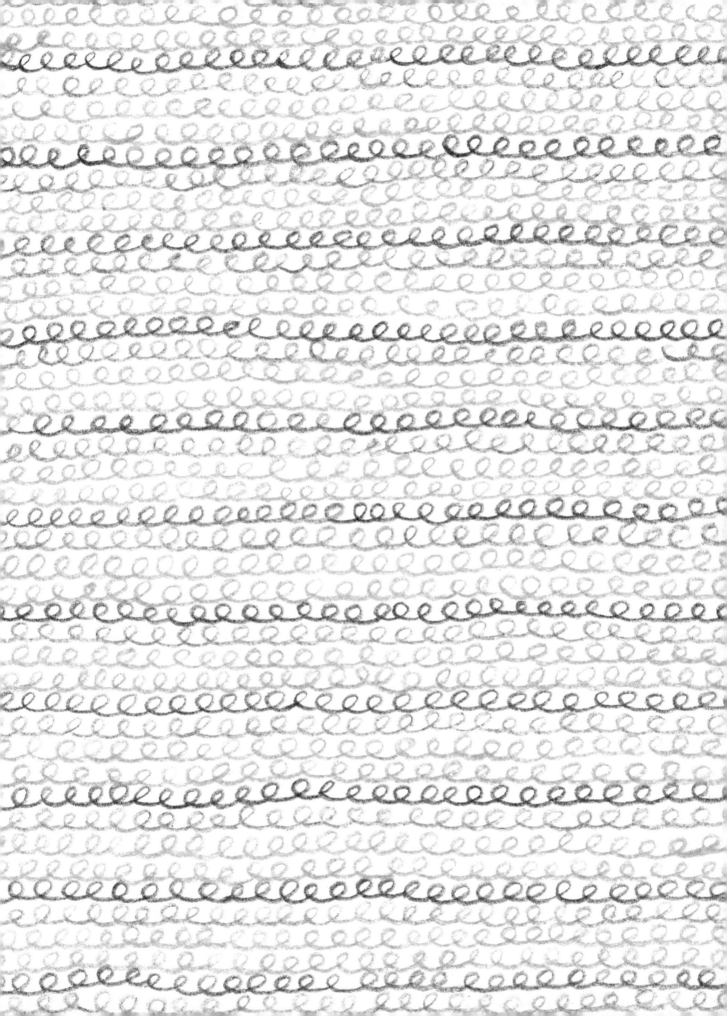